Nightshade Publishing™ Presents

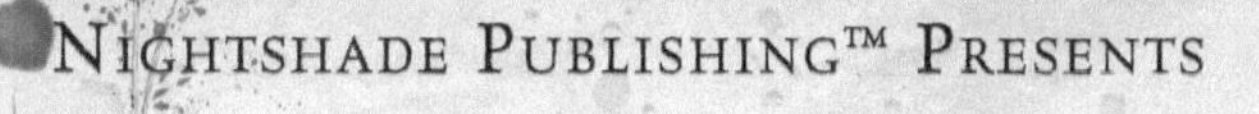

Of Ink & Paper

XANNA RENAE
WILLOW WHITEHEAD
ABRAHAM VILA
KAYLA WHITTLE
NATASHA ALVA
KRISTEN BAZEN
HANNAH CARTER
MIRIAM STUART
ANNE J. HILL
KATIE FITZGERALD

First Edition May 2023

ISBN 979-8-9850823-4-0 (paperback)
ISBN 979-8-9850823-5-7 (ebook)

Published by Nightshade Publishing
NightshadePublishing.com™

OF Ink & PAPER

Other Works by Nightshade Publishing™

Through the Violet Redwoods

The Willow Tree Swing

Story List

* Story contains mentions of sexual assault

A Letter to my Lost

Xanna Renae

She ran her fingertips over the worn paper, yellow along the edges and scratched on the face from dragging the dry nib of her pen several times over. She tried tracing her sentences before setting them in ink. They evaded her. Leaving her wondering how to start the words that longed to burst from her chest like a dove in a cage.

A few pairs of footsteps circled and echoed about her in the old library, dust covered most of the thousands of aged books that lined most of the shelves, and the rest of them were filled with modern tellings of stories whose origins were long forgotten. All of these words were able to be written but the ones inside of her refused to let her alone and be freed.

There were a million different ways that one could start a letter.

But she couldn't find any of them as she footslogged through her head.

So she stood and started over to the grand shelves to the left. She forgot to set the pen down beside her bag and paper. It twirled about in her fingers. Her legs enjoyed the last bits of light that the grand windows let in. The skirt she wore hit just at her knees, a scandalous bit of fashion that was making its way into the world.

The worn leather spines were refreshing on her fingertips. One at a time she plucked a book free, skimming the words over the course of a few pages. Hoping she'd find her own words there. She found only the words of others, which was to be expected.

Perhaps the words escaped her because writing a letter to someone who was lost was pointless. Her mind couldn't conjure the words to fit her feelings in the end, there was no point. The recipient was gone.

She moved from classic literature to poems, and still found nothing. Art books held no answers, nor the atlases— aside from giving her more places she could run away and hide in. The coasts looked promising.

They had spoken about going there once. Buying a house painted a deep green with pine along the edges. A small kitchen and space for a family to grow. Whispered promises of dancing with the waves that crashed against the cliffs on breaths that the wind had stolen from her.

The thought stopped her from making the next stride.

Maybe—just maybe their breaths had traveled to all the places they wanted to see?

That was a comforting thought. They *had* made it.

The pen almost fell from her hands. She needed to tell him that.

Her skirt fluttered and flapped behind her as the leather shoes she wore clacked upon the marble floors like horses in a race.

She dipped her pen into the little well of ink she had picked off of the librarian's desk and scrawled the date in the upper corner.

Now there was nothing left to do but bleed.

In the Eye

Willow Whitehead

The words start to flow onto the page,
Is this what contentment feels like?

The noise in my mind starts to dim,
With every word I type.

My head feels light:
The pressure that was building is gone now.

The clack of the keys,
Sound like rain, falling on a sunny day

The calm starts to seep in.

Will I be able to sleep tonight?

Now that the words are no longer stuck inside my mind,

Will my thoughts finally be still?

Even if they are not,

This moment, this short time of peace, is all I dare to

request.

Nights of Ink

Abraham Vila

I always wait
for the moon to appear
high above the velvet sky.
Her bright halo
with her delicate magic;
and the soft, flickering light
of a little candle
are the only companions
of my imagination.
I play some quiet music,
meaningful,

soulful;

while the nib dances

over the white sea of paper.

The hand has ways

to drive the words deeper

with only its gesture.

Some nights

the soft cadence of a piano played long-ago

leads my hand to paint in words

the beauty of your hazel eyes.

Other nights the jazz

takes my mind away

and I wander and pace the room,

oft, in dreams.

I see the most beautiful verses,

the most disquieting rhymes,

but when the day rises

and I try to write

my hand is dead.

It stops

because

only under the silvery halo of Diana

am I able to write these verses.

Ink

Kayla Whittle

A llow me to taste your ink, if you'd like to enter my library," the vampire said as soon as I crossed the threshold. Moonlight-speckled silver in the gaps between the heavy curtains covering the windows in the front room. Rows of bookshelves stood at attention in the dark beside my host, waiting for me to pay his fee. My eyes burned and blisters throbbed—I knew the rumors I'd followed into the forest were true. The vampire's library contained more information than most humans could fathom, but his knowledge came at a price. Most paid it with their lives on the journey; there were many things living within the trees ready to tear and bite and lead travelers astray. Arriving alive was half the goal.

I nodded, and he held out his hand. His palm was white, unnaturally smooth, no wrinkles. No lifelines.

"It only stings for a moment," he said, voice smooth, soft—a quiet reassurance, like my father's had once been, steady, chasing away monsters I now willingly sought.

A sharp pinch precluded the dull ache that crawled up my arm, through my chest. I looked at the vampire, startled to feel the warm press of my mother's embrace. The ink pooled on my skin, dragging memories forward so vividly I could nearly see them in the sheen clinging to my skin. I flinched at the memory of my brother's hands shoving at my shoulders, turned toward the sweet scent of cinnamon, tried to back away from the cloying taste of blood on my tongue. The vampire held me fast.

Thick globs of black, depths glistening purple and midnight blue, smeared across my skin. A cosmos of memory caught in the flickering candlelight, part of the story that made up my life until the moment I'd reached the library. The ink rolled down my forearm, looped around my wrist, and then dug into the vampire's hand. A bitter tang clung to the back of my throat. The memories remained, but now part of them belonged to him. My mother's goodbye stung a little less deeply. My father's indifference was shared. I thought back to my brother's sneer, when I'd fallen and bled before I left. It hurt less, as if someone had rubbed the raw edges of those moments grey. I felt worse knowing someone had tasted the broken pieces of me.

"Salty," the vampire said, pulling his tongue across his teeth. His eyes had gone dark as the ink that'd disappeared between us. "You taste like salt and smoke. A hint of cinnamon."

When stressed, my mother baked. When pressed, I'd fled.

"Stay the night," the vampire said. "Search if you'd like. Don't set the collection on fire."

He left me with a row of unused candles, walking into the shadowed stacks as I rubbed at my wrist. I could still feel the slight ooze of ink against my skin. That memory remained sharp.

I woke with pages crushed beneath my cheek and the vampire tapping on my shoulder. Night had fallen again and found me in a deeper, darker place. My dreams had urged me homeward, taunting me with a warmth that wouldn't exist if I failed to find answers in the library.

I'd turned pages until my hands cramped, read until my vision blurred and smeared and failed me.

"Will you remain in my library?" the vampire asked.

"Yes," I said, offering him my hand. "I'm not finished."

Together we watched the ink spiral down beneath his

skin. More of my story, but some of the older pages, when my feet had always been dirty and my stomach always full. My ears rang with old laughter, coated sour on the edges with the pleading I'd done before I'd left. Begging my family to listen, to understand. When he released me, I couldn't recall the exact words I'd said, or track the tension written into the lines of my family as they'd let me go.

"Stay the night," the vampire said, patting my hand, just once. "Remember that one day your ink will run dry."

I swallowed down the panic that rose to meet his warning. When the ink was gone, I would have nothing left to pay, and he would force me out of his library. Back into that cold, dangerous forest; back to my loneliness. The story of my life wasn't so long, so far; I didn't have much time before my welcome would run out. I needed to find my answers quickly; I had no other choice. Nothing to go back to if I arrived emptyhanded.

I turned back to the books, finding some comfort in their indifference toward who held them.

"What question brought you here?" the vampire asked on the third night. He'd found me deep in the library, down a spiraling stairway across from an echoing chamber. A cramp locked my neck and my eyes burned for sunlight that couldn't be found there.

"If I tell you, could you help me find my answers?"

I asked, pressing my lips together, tight, when he glanced away. I'd known I'd be doing this alone; the stories I'd followed never mentioned any assistance offered by my host. Still, I realized how nice it was to have someone sit beside me, someone who might listen.

"I look after the books," the vampire explained. "I don't look into them."

He waited, dark eyes fixed on mine, as if I'd promised him a story.

"I need to find a way for them to understand me," I said, flushing under his attention. From frustration, and shame, and anger that I had been forced to feel ashamed. "Then I can go."

"Who is it that brought you here?" The vampire asked.

"My family," I answered. My brother, whose lips had peeled back as he'd shouted at me to fix myself or never return. My mother, who would have me shove the truth away inside me, deep enough to rot and fester. My father, who had already started the slow process of pretending I didn't exist.

"Myself," I added later. Because through time and distance, the weeks that had passed since I'd left home, my despair had dulled into determination. Because beneath the hard words and rough hands and confusion, all I really wanted was a way to claw back to happiness.

I stared at one of my open books while we held hands.

That night, the ink stabbed deep.

"What don't they understand?" the vampire asked a few days later. "Would I?"

He'd brought another chair to sit beside mine, and had stood to relight one of my candles when it flickered and faded in a draft sneaking between the endless bookcases. There were depths to this library I would never touch, a perpetual itch at the back of my neck.

"I don't know," I admitted. "I've only just begun to understand it myself."

It had been horrific and gratifying all at once, to realize something that had always been a part of me. To put into words how I felt, or more essentially what I didn't feel. The relief that came with speaking truth aloud and then, everything that had come afterward. The screaming upset that had never belonged to me.

"I can taste it in your ink," he said, rubbing a hand across his thin lips. "I'm putting together the story of you, out of order. There are too many paragraphs still missing."

I leaned back, wood creaking beneath me in a squeal, a questioning squeal. Smoothed a hand over one of the crumbling books tucked into my lap, filled with stories about other families and relationships and children and expectations.

"My parents told me it was good to be different," I

said. "They meant someone who stood out as a leader or inventor or storyteller. Not the kind of different when you could love someone, and love them well, but part of you shrivels inside whenever your lips touch. Where you aren't sure you'll ever be comfortable with kissing, or more."

They hadn't understood, because I hardly had the words to understand it myself. I didn't need an explanation, but they did, and in one of these books I'd find the right words. A good way of telling it. A way to fix things, when I refused to see it as a way to fix me. A way to make them understand.

"She left me when I told her," I said to the vampire. "I loved her but that wasn't enough for her to stay. My family wants me to do anything to get her back. Pretend like that conversation never happened. It's important to our social standing. Important to them, how others see our family. I'm the one ruining our reputation because my wife left me. Because I won't give her children. Because I rarely want to touch her."

The vampire exhaled. His hand flexed against the armrest.

"Are you comfortable, when we—"

"Oh, yes," I said, turning back to the books and holding out my hand. "A friendly hand, I've never minded."

The ink ran slow, days later. Weak, greyer than the vampire's frown. The memories dredged up the feel of rain against my scalp. The sweet taste of apples harvested from my family's orchard. I remembered a different, smaller hand, enveloped in mine before pulling away. It felt as if a sheet had been hung between me and my past. I could still see it and remember it well, but, out of sight, it mattered less. I didn't know if that was because of me, or the vampire; I decided I didn't care.

"You don't have many stories left to share," the vampire said, licking his lips.

"I need to stay," I said. "I need answers."

Time had slipped away from me, slick as the darkness fading beneath the vampire's skin. My nails dug into my wrist as if the sharp pain would draw out more ink, add a few extra chapters to my life. Beyond us, the library continued onward and backward, to shelves filled with novels and textbooks I hadn't touched, notebooks and loose pages I needed to read. I'd skimmed hundreds of stories, read thousands of spines and still had no explanation to give to my family. I had no way to fix things in a way that would bring back my wife.

"This library holds much, but not everything," the vampire said. "Many leave satisfied, but some never look in the right place."

My breath hitched, mouth drying with the first flares of a panic I'd hoped to bury somewhere in those faded memories. Failure loomed and more than anything, I felt utterly alone.

"I don't mean to say it's any fault of yours," the vampire told me, stark and calm as a period perfectly placed at the end of a run-on sentence. "Sometimes it's the people my visitors left behind who most need to pay the library a visit."

Two evenings later, the candles burned low, and no ink flowed between us when the vampire took my hand. I swallowed down my disappointment, abandoning the last of my books on a tabletop to gather dust until a new patron arrived. I'd heard stories of visitors who'd overstayed their welcome—or rather, stories of those who never left the library alive. It was time for me to leave.

The vampire led me past sections I'd already sorted through and sections I'd left untouched. Dread built in my chest, dragged at my ankles. I'd found stories of others like me, some who'd found love and some who'd never wanted it, some who had families supporting them and others who'd gone on alone. There was no why to it, no reasoning—that was just the way those people were, the way their lives had been lived.

Moonlight gathered in the library's front room, peeking through the old curtains.

"I'm sorry to have bothered you," I told the vampire on his threshold.

"Did you?" He asked, thin lips curving.

I thought of the stories I'd read and the people in them,

and wondered if my mother or father or brother turned those pages, if they would see through to the truth of me. They'd see I wasn't someone waiting to be fixed. They'd see there was more to a person than changing themselves to preserve a legacy.

I exhaled. My family could find their own way to the library, if they were willing to risk the journey. My work was done, when it hadn't been my burden to bear to begin with.

"You may return when you have more stories to share," the vampire said. He squeezed my hand before letting me go. "Though I hope you will find my library bearing different questions. In the meantime, less salt would do well for your ink, I think."

I smiled at him again then went out into the world and left the library behind.

No Words

Natasha Alva

I can never rewrite the days of tearing myself apart, with no remorse or help from anyone.

It has been days of staring at the ceiling, lost in translation with nothing to write on.

Everything I make seems wrong in the eyes of the public. I do not stand a chance.

Every word that I write goes to rubble.

Every idea I make goes ignored or is used by others with the audacity to claim it as theirs.

It is hard to speak up, especially when I am beneath them.

Following rules keep them happy, bending them results

in disagreements, and breaking them leads to punishment.

Full of doubts, I would rather drown myself within the emptiness inside me.

Why is falling into the abyss easier than making its mark on the pages?

Can I at least get praise and validation for once on my efforts?

When can my masterpiece become the iconic?

I am out of words and melodies, writing scribbles and playing off-key tunes on my piano.

All the sheets of paper are scattered on the floor, ready to be thrown away.

I have no one with me, I am alone.

There are no words for giving the motivation in standing up for myself.

There are no words in having the guts to continue my story.

There are no words to make it all better.

Will I still have the chance to work it out in the future?

All I know is there are no words in believing that I can make it, for now.

A Teacup of Stories

Kristen Bazen

A dipper full of stars
Drawn from the lake.
A secret note on Mars
Found by blessed mistake.

A net to catch the sun
Made of silken strings.
A race that can be won
Riding on butterfly wings.

A child with a song
Healing war's deep pain.

A sword of silver strong

Humming honor's refrain.

A ladder of purple lilies

Hanging from a cloud.

A fiery herd of noble fillies

Smoking from nostrils proud.

A merry voice of wind

Playing tag with the bees.

A lion scaled and finned

Leaping through wild seas.

A garden sown with deeds

That are pruned into flowers.

A jacket spun from seeds

Sprouted in crystal towers.

A ball gown made of light

Captured from sunset skies.

A tree with leaves of white

Withered by the moonrise.

A captain with a key

Plucked from an oyster.

A princess who must flee

Through a cathedral cloister.

A canoe built with ice
Sliding through storms.
An idea that flickers twice
Before it slowly reforms.

A teacup of stories
Held between my fingers.
I yearn to explore these
But indecision lingers.

Which idea I'll choose
I cannot yet say.
But if I long peruse
They'll all fly away.

House of Shadows

Hannah Carter

Proserpina lived in the shadows.

As an author, she lived in the shadow of her best-selling mother.

As a witch, she lived in the shadow of her elder sister, who had blossomed at an early age and decided to hone her talent into a craft.

And now, in Proserpina's own life, she lived in the shadow of the *Incident*.

A stray brown strand of hair came undone from her bun, and she tucked it back inside with one hand while the other held her pen. She stared at the blank page in front of her and sucked in a deep breath.

Her fingers shook as she lowered the ink-stained tip to the page.

The tears hit the page before she could make a single mark.

Proserpina choked on the first round of tears and dropped the pen so she could wipe her eyes. Her soul trembled inside her, and her breathing hitched. A *pang* seized her heart, and she closed her eyes to try and muddle through it.

No. She couldn't do it. She just couldn't do it. Not when the shadows threatened to choke her.

She fled her study before the darkness that clung to the walls, to her writing, to her soul, could suffocate her.

She wandered down the hallway, a ghost in her own house. She'd pulled all the curtains closed to keep any sunlight from creeping in and casting any more ghastly shadows. Her tiny cottage could only stand to be haunted by one resident ghost, and she had taken up occupancy.

Maybe she'd make herself some tea and then go back and try to write. Perhaps she'd pull out her old typewriter, to keep herself in check. So she never caused another Incident again.

Once in the kitchen, Proserpina put the kettle on the stove and lit the burner with a match. If her older sister Jupiter had been there, Jupey could have snapped her fingers and set it ablaze. But Proserpina's magic didn't work like that. She needed a conduit, and, unfortunately, her pen was hers.

And look what you did with it. Ensnared thousands of unsuspecting people. Made them fake fans because you enchanted them. It's your uncontrolled magic, not your talent, that makes you irresistible.

The cold words, a collection of memories, threatened to pull Proserpina down. She could almost feel them around her neck like the hands of the person that had uttered them.

She sucked in a breath. Her teacup rattled as her hands trembled. *She* was the ghost in her house—so why did those words, *that person*—haunt her?

Tea in hand, Proserpina wandered back to her office. It had taken her over a year to work up the nerve to even consider the prospect of writing after the Incident. Even now, the only thing that really drove her was the tiny ember in her soul, the ashes of a fire that once burned with words, worlds, and paper. Back when creativity seemed to burst from her, to seep from her fingertips onto the page. Everything had come so easy—

Like magic.

Proserpina studied the murky liquid inside her cup and held back her equally hot tears. "You're a fraud," she whispered to her reflection. "Your words aren't actually good. It's all just spells and charms you didn't know you were using." The girl inside the tea's reflection didn't respond, but she did seem open to some more insults.

She typically was.

"Even with all that untapped magic, you still couldn't write anything half as good as your mother. And she did it all by herself, without even a stitch of magic in her veins. Raw talent and skill. Who are you to think you acquired any of that?"

Proserpina sighed and rolled her eyes. Her own reflection wasn't the best conversationalist, but she didn't have anyone else. She'd pushed everyone away after the Incident, locked her doors, let their letters go unread. Let them think she died; all the better, really.

Death would be better than reality. That she was twenty-three, washed up and past her writing prime at such a young age. Never again to have any prospects, any hope, any future.

So why did she sit down once again in her blasted chair? Why did she put down her tea and position her fingers on the typewriter keys? And why, oh why, did Proserpina even bother to type out that first dreadful sentence:

"Once upon a time…"

She scowled. No—too trite.

She rolled the paper down to the next line and sent it back to the beginning with a lovely ching from the machine.

"Two children lived in the forest…"

No, that was no beginning. She needed something exciting.

"And it came to pass…"

"Have you ever wanted to live in a forest?"

"Bubbling streams and chirping birds…"

Attempt after attempt Proserpina crumpled and discarded. The shadows upon her curtains shifted as the day wore on, and she came no closer to a new manuscript than when she'd begun.

More bits of hair tumbled loose from Proserpina's bun and fell in her eyes. Nothing! Nothing, nothing, nothing she did ever turned out right.

She ripped the latest monstrosity from the typewriter's grasp and shredded it with her own hands.

"Why—aren't—you—good—enough?!" She punctuated each word with a satisfying rip as she tore up her mistakes.

She let out a rebel scream and let bits of paper flutter down to the ground and settle like snow at her feet.

If only she could erase the Incident as well as she could these abominations. If only she could go back, see the maliciousness that hid behind the blue eyes as the stranger approached her…if only she could warn her past self not to be drawn in by his empty praises and see through the manipulation.

He'd been drawn in by her charms—the magic kind, as she didn't possess many others to speak of. But she'd drawn him in with her bespelled handwritten prose, and been immediately smitten. Not that she knew that at the time—

no, she'd only figured out he'd been enchanted later—

A knock came on the door.

Proserpina jerked her head up. Her breath hitched. No—he couldn't possibly know where she lived now. She'd moved, packed up her entire life after the Incident, only told her family her new location. And with every letter that came, she regretted even that, the small reminder that she still lived and people cared to make sure she continued to do so…

The knocking at the door intensified.

She crawled from her office and down the hallway. Perhaps she could peer through the glass before she would be required to interact with the person—

"Prosey?" A tall man with untamed, floppy brown hair stood at the door and spoke loudly through the glass. He wore a navy jacket and matching slacks, the uniform of the magic school where he taught. "What are you doing on the floor?"

Heat flashed through her cheeks. Embarrassment mingled with anger as she glared at his chest, unable to meet his brown eyes. "Go away, Leo."

"You didn't answer my letters, and your family hasn't seen you in two months." Leo jiggled the doorknob. "They were worried about you."

"Then tell them to come." Proserpina sat on the floor like a forgotten childhood doll, discarded after years of hard play.

"Let me in, Prosey." Leo held up a bag. "I brought food."

She debated. What were the chances that she could get the food and shove Leo down the steps at the same time…?

Probably not good.

She could at least survive a few minutes of socialization if it saved her from having to cook.

Still sitting, she scooted back into the hallway with the intention to fully merge with the shadows and become invisible. "Fine. Let yourself in." Hopefully, he would just put the food on the table and leave.

Leo must have whispered a spell, because an audible click resounded through the room as the latch unlocked. He squeezed in, all six-foot-something and wiry limbs.

"I think it's a fine day for a picnic, don't you?" He grabbed a coral throw blanket from the back of the couch as he approached her.

"I don't want to go outside," Proserpina grumbled. She wanted to stay here in the shadows.

Forever.

"That's fine." Leo unfurled the blanket on the ground beside her and sat down to unload his find. "Your mother sent food. Rice, grilled chicken, that yellow fruit you like…"

"Cocabu fruit." From her childhood home on the island. A rare find on the continent of Solis, unless one was close to the ocean borders.

Proserpina reached inside the bag and began to peel the fruit with her ink-stained hands. Juice dribbled out onto her skin, and she raised it to her mouth to lick it off—but Leo intercepted her first.

He grasped her fingers in one hand and brought them up to his lips.

"Stop, stop!" Proserpina squealed as he sucked the juice. "You're so gross, Leo!"

"It got a laugh, didn't it?" Her fingers still rested inside his mouth, and she giggled.

"Only because it tickles. You're so weird!"

"I know." Leo's eyes lost a bit of their mischievous sparkle.

She sobered as he left tiny kisses on the pads of her fingers…and the inside of her wrist.

"I'm sorry." Leo whispered against her skin. "All teasing aside. It's my fault."

Perhaps a more genteel girl would have tried to assuage his self-blame, but Proserpina had spent a very dark period of her life blaming him.

No use stopping now.

"It was."

Leo flinched. "Don't hold back."

"Well, you said it first." Proserpina slipped her hand from his and tucked it into the folds of her dress. She may have had tears about her writing left to shed, but she didn't have any more tears to cry over the Incident. Just cold, hard facts. "But you asked me on a date and stood me up. I waited and waited, and if you had kept your promise and not left me waiting, there never would have been an empty seat for Augustine to claim."

"I know." Leo ducked his head. He let the silence linger between them until he reached for the food. The crinkling of the bag sounded far too loud in the silence. "I can't apologize enough, Prosey. And if you never forgive me, that's fair. But forgive yourself, please."

Proserpina chewed on the inside of her cheek and focused on the muffled clunk she could hear inside her head if she got just enough skin-to-teeth ratio. At least it gave her something to concentrate on instead of the voices inside her head.

"I mean it." Leo sniffed. She had cried all her tears about the Incident, but perhaps he hadn't. "You have to come out of your house. You have to write again. It's everything you've ever been passionate about, ever since we were little."

Proserpina swallowed. "I don't—"

"You've always had a book or a notebook in your hand. Even when I first met you, when you came to school to visit your sister for the first time. On the tour, whenever there was a lull, you'd pull out your book and stick your nose right in it..." Leo looked down at the styrofoam container and jabbed it a few times with a plastic fork. The scent of the chicken and rice lingered in the air, potent and sweet.

Proserpina cleared her throat and glanced at her heap of unread books, piled precariously in stacks on her bookshelves. So many worlds, things her eyes and mind were hungry for. But the words there—they mocked her.

Your works aren't fit to join us, their spines seemed to hiss. *Your books can't sit with us here.*

Proserpina blinked. Did she feel the first pinpricks of tears behind her lids? No. Impossible. She'd sworn to herself. She had no more tears left to cry over this stupid Incident.

"And—I remember when you first let me read it. You were so nervous and shy about it…" Leo stabbed the lid so hard the fork went straight into it. "You couldn't even make eye contact when you asked me to look over it. But I loved it, because…it felt like you'd let me into a personal part of your heart. A place you didn't let everyone go."

Proserpina pursed her lips. "It turns out that sometimes I let the wrong people into that place." She turned her head. "But it doesn't matter. I don't think I'll ever write again."

Leo stabbed the container again. "You have to—"

"I do not!" The words exploded from within her. She could almost feel the dam inside her heart explode with the weight of all the emotions that had built up, not just today and her failed attempts, but ever since the Incident. "I'm a bad writer, Leo." She stormed over to the bookshelf and picked up her first published novel. Her debut.

She tossed it to the ground. It slid closer to Leo, and she pointed at the offending item. "That book got published solely because it is a witch's conduit. I poured my magic into it, and it charmed my readers. I don't have talent. I didn't even realize I'd enchanted it until—" Proserpina licked her dry lips. She could feel the cracked skin underneath her tongue. "—until Augustine told me."

"He's a *liar.*"

"He's many things, but he was right about that!" Proserpina gestured furiously to her writing. "I'm a bad writer who only got published because of magic. And I'm a bad witch because I let my magic leak out." Augustine had told her that much, almost on a daily basis.

As a writer himself, he'd wormed his way into her life. Tried to teach her all the mechanics she'd failed to properly grasp. But she still used the wrong words, had flimsy plots, stereotypical characters, and love interests that all seemed a little too much like Leo in retrospect. Her worldbuilding lacked substance and her stories were too short. Augustine could teach her those subjects. He'd published a successful thriller series. He'd been in her spot before, an aspiring, up-and-coming newbie with one pathetic attempt at a novel released. He simply wanted to help her.

He only wanted to help her with a lot of things.

Like their relationship.

He only wanted to help her loosen up. Help show her how a girlfriend would treat their boyfriend if they really liked them.

That meant that Augustine had to push her limits. She'd let him kiss her more than she felt comfortable with, let his hands wander in places she hadn't felt appropriate. He was her first boyfriend, and he knew it. He'd used that against her once when she'd tried to express her feelings.

"You're just inexperienced and scared," Augustine whispered. "Just like in your writing. Just like in your magic."

So she'd stuffed her emotions down. Maybe she was just a bit too uptight…maybe she did need to thank him for all the advice he'd offered, all the assistance he'd given.

And then—the Incident.

The night he'd pushed their relationship much, much farther than she wanted.

She'd fought him. She'd screamed. But she couldn't protect herself with magic without a conduit. And her home rested far away from her parents, siblings, and friends for anyone to hear her cry.

Augustine always got what he wanted, and Proserpina hadn't even been able to use her words as weapons in the midst of her terror.

But Augustine had.

"No one will believe you if you tell them." His large hand covered her mouth and kept her pinned to the ground.

His weight hurt as he leaned into her. "Besides, this is your fault. You ensorcelled me. Used your magical words to make me obsessed with you, you witch. Just like all your fans."

Proserpina's breath came faster. She clutched at the high neck of her dress and struggled to get air. The world spun— she staggered into the bookshelf and caused it to rattle.

Bad writer.

Bad witch.

Bad *person*.

"I'm horrible," she whispered. Her heart hurt as it thumped inside her chest. It felt like it actually collided with her ribs and might crack one of them.

"Hey." Leo leapt across the blanket and staggered a few steps until he regained his balance by her side, the maimed styrofoam box forgotten. "No, you're not. You're not. Look at me."

He cupped her cheeks, but Proserpina's eyes darted everywhere. She couldn't look at him. She couldn't gaze into the depths of his soul, couldn't have him probe hers, or else he would see what Augustine always saw. What everyone would see.

Worthless. Phony. Fraud. Ensorceller.

She'd cut Augustine off, moved, and asked her sister to place a million and one protective charms over the new house. But no matter how hard she tried to cut off her emotions, those tainted thoughts and recollections still haunted her like shadows in her mind.

"I'm sorry," Leo whispered. "I am so sorry. I will never forgive myself. I should have been there—I should have, I know—all those pitiful excuses I gave you at first for why I didn't show up seem hollow now. I'm so, so sorry. I will never forgive myself for not being there for you. But you need to forgive yourself. Please. Please?" He wrapped her in a hug and pulled her close. She squirmed, unsure if she liked the way his warmth crept through her, the way his heartbeat melded with hers. "Nothing that monster said or did to you is true or reflects on you. He…" Leo sighed, and his breath ruffled the few tiny hairs that had slipped out of her bun. "He was just jealous of you, I'm sure. Because your books are magical, Prosey. But not because they're your conduit. It's because they're your heart and soul, laid bare for all the world to see."

Proserpina's bottom lip quivered. Her nose flared, too, and her teeth clattered.

"They're special because they're yours. You're so… so you. So charming—and I'm not talking about spells or enchantments, either. You're endearing and sarcastic, prickly but sweet, and you love—my word, if you just talk to your family, you'd see it—you are so loved and you are love. You have an unfathomable capacity to love, but you hold yourself back so much just because you're scared of how others might react, or scared because you don't know if you could ever say everything that's in your heart properly."

Proserpina's knees buckled. If Leo's arms hadn't been wrapped around her, she would have fallen right there. But all she could do was borrow from his strength, which he freely lent to her.

She buried her face in his shoulder and stained the fabric with her tears.

But these weren't tears from the Incident.

These felt like tears of being seen.

Of being known.

"I've read every book you've ever written—even the ones that haven't been published. Even that short story about the old dog that adopted a kitten—" Leo chuckled and pressed his nose into her bun. "—Prosey, that blowhard was jealous of you. Threatened by you, too. Because he knew that you had something that came effortlessly. The ability to be you, to share your heart and soul with people. And he wanted to squash that and you in every way he knew possible. But you're still here. You're still you. You're still loved just as much, and—would you please answer some letters every once in a while? Just so we know you're alive?"

Proserpina laughed, made wet by her tears and emotions. She wiped at her mouth and nodded. "I'll try."

"Good." Leo's grip tightened. "I'm sorry. I'm so sorry I let you down."

"I...I know." Proserpina's voice trembled.

"Please don't be scared of yourself anymore," Leo murmured. "Don't rob the world of your heart because one monster tried to murder it."

Proserpina sniffed. Nodded. "I'll try."

The shadows in her office lengthened as Proserpina sank down to her messy desk. Leo hadn't stayed much longer, but he had promised to come back the next day and see what she'd written. And he promised to bring food, and—if she didn't mind—Proserpina's sister, Jupiter, as well.

The last vestiges of day created one final moment of splendor outside Proserpina's window as they turned the sky a brilliant orange. Silhouettes of black trees reached out toward the sun, like they were desperate to stop its descent.

How could a world where things like the Incident happened be so pretty?

But then again, Leo existed in this world, too. And he happened to be far too handsome for it as well.

If she could work past her writer's block, perhaps it might finally be time to forgive Leo for his mistakes, as well.

"I swear, I never meant to be late. I overslept, and I know that's an awful excuse, but it's true, and I'm so sorry."

That had been Leo's first excuse, which she had brushed off. If he'd really cared, he wouldn't have been an hour late. And by then, she'd already been reeled in by Augustine's glib tongue and friendly demeanor. The fact that he could hold a conversation about literature.

But the truth had come out later, about Augustine's sleazy ways and Leo's excuses. Leo hadn't merely overslept; he'd overslept because he was a night owl who couldn't keep a proper bedtime if his life depended on it. But he'd been up late that night studying for his finals, because he'd devoted all his evening hours chatting with her through their mirrors.

Proserpina jabbed a sliver of cocabu fruit with her fork. If he'd merely been late, she would have forgiven him once all the angst wore off. She knew him well enough to know him, and he never claimed punctuality as a strong suit.

What had taken her longer to work through was that his mistake had led to a huge mistake on her part, and, therefore, the Incident.

But really…

Maybe it was time to forgive him…and herself.

The typewriter sat in front of her on her desk. It was a protection from her powers, a wall between her heart and her readers.

She could hear it mock her, its words echoing the sentiments of the books from her bookshelf earlier, the insecurities Augustine had preyed upon. "You're not a good enough witch to stop your magic from creeping into your stories, and you're not a good enough author to write without it. You're nothing, Proserpina. Nothing but a shadow of a woman."

She tucked her toes inside the hem of her dress. Sucked in a breath.

She could stay stuck in her misery forever.

Or...

She opened the drawer and pulled out a pen and notebook. One she'd used back as a young teenager. It curved and bulged with the weight of imaginary worlds, stuffed full of childish, handwritten notes, and tiny drawings in the margin where Leo had taken it upon himself to illustrate her words to the best of his lackluster ability.

She tucked the pen between her fingers. A spark of magic jumped from her skin as she did and made the little instrument glow.

Did she dare?

"You're a shadow of an author, a shadow of a witch, a shadow of a girl," the typewriter reminded her.

She picked it up and shoved it in her closet. With a slam of the doors, she silenced its taunts.

Daylight drained from the room, coating Proserpina in darkness, but inside her heart, she felt a spark of light.

She would not be a shadow.

She would illuminate the world.

Proserpina took a deep breath, opened to a fresh page, and pressed the pen to paper.

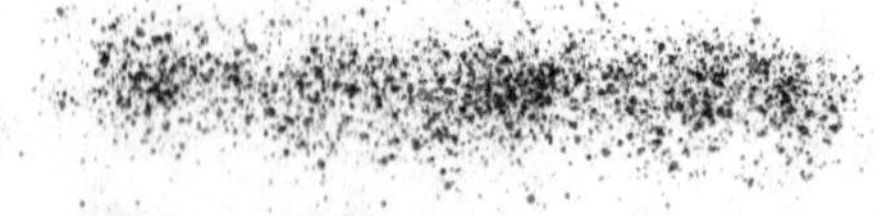

Generation of Words

Miriam Stuart

There once was an Idea
who married an Imagination.
Time passed, and Idea, happy and proud,
birthed a beautiful Sentence.
Sentence grew up and married Phrase
and Paragraph was born soon after.
Paragraph eloped with Passage,
and for a period of time, did not have offspring.
But many weeks later,
Paragraph brought forth Chapter.
Chapter, an only child, grew older
and realized how lonesome he was.

There were none like him, not even one.

With a broken heart, he sadly thought

"There is no purpose for me,

I'm all this story's got."

But then he remembered the wise words

his great-grandmother Idea had spoken:

"Our family has a story to tell

though it may take generations to form."

From then on, his heart was gladdened,

because he knew it would not be long

before another Section came along.

Muse

Anne J. Hill

Oh, sweet muse, hear my cry
    Grant me inspirations this day
    This book desperately needs done
So, lead me on my way."

Though the writer knew not
That he was actually quite near
And the kind muse she spoke to
Had freckled skin and pointy ears

On her shoulder he sat
Muse, rather proud of himself

She was his author
And he was her elf

He patted her head
And whispered in her ear
All the wonderful ideas
She needed to hear

You see, Muse was picked
Just for her by his kind
One elf for one year
With a writer in mind

So proudly he sat
Watching her type away
And the joy in her eyes
Made his tiny heart sway

Little Muse grew content
His eyes drifting closed
And atop her shoulder there
He started to doze

When he finally awoke, he saw
She'd closed her writing docs
And on the couch now she lay

Watching the magical box

But worst of all were the trolls
Dancing on her head with delight
Muse curtly pulled his bow
And marched toward the sorry sight

He lifted arrow to string
"Who are you?" he begged
"Leave her alone, or
To the dogs you'll be fed."

"I am Net," said one troll
As he laughed and sneered
"And I am Flix,"
The other one jeered

Muse shook his head in fury
"She needs real rest!
Don't you see the way
You both are making her stressed?"

"The magical box is rest,"
Flix said in fiendish wile
"Might even give an idea,"
Net sang with mischief in his smile

Muse had enough of that
And rang his arrow true
A warning shot indeed
It zipped between the two

"Yes, it can be rest
But not the kind she needs
At the moment, at least
And not with your crazy deeds."

The Fairies of Rest
Through the window they flew
With wonder and grace
As if summoned on cue

"Ah, at last! Save our author,"
Muse pled on his knees
The fairies scooped up those trolls
Tossing them to the trees

The little elf sighed
As his author stood to leave
And out the door she went
On a walk in the breeze

The fairies fluttered after
Helping her truly rest
Giving her mind a break
From epic tales and quests

Content again, Muse sat
Perched upon her shoulder top
Preparing for his next task
Collecting inspiration and thought

The trolls would soon come back
But for then, they stayed away
Bothering another helpless author
Until their return the following day

And every morning, Muse scolded
And fought with them all
Until the author's mind was taken
And someone would withdraw

Sometimes Muse rose victorious
The words written with determination
Or the Fairies of Rest did their best
To refocus her attention

Sometimes though, the trolls prevailed

And then nothing got done
No real rest to be had
And all songs left unsung

But everyday, Muse stood fast
Against the trolls, Net and Flix
And magical boxes of different sizes
Nothing was too hard for him to fix

Character Driven

Katie Fitzgerald

I'm tying my sneakers by the front door when the alarm on my phone goes off. 'DEADLINE TOMORROW' reads the accompanying message. My column is due in less than thirty-six hours, and I need to get started. Just two miles, I tell myself, as I step into the brisk autumn air and begin a gentle jog. After that, I'll glue my butt to the chair.

The sun is just rising as I exit the cul-de-sac, pass the bus stop, and turn in the direction of the park. My mind wanders, and suddenly, at the corner, she's beside me, matching my pace.

Her long swinging ponytail first appears reddish, then turns several shades of brown before settling on a dirty blonde. She smiles expectantly. "Hi."

"Hello… Lois?" I venture.

"Louise," she says. "Wait. Actually, Zoe."

"Zoe." I nod. "That's a good name."

"I'm Zoe Lewis, and I'm a—" She looks to me to complete her thought. I'm about to say I don't know, but as we pass the playground it comes to me.

"A preschool teacher," I tell her. "You're a preschool teacher because you like kids and you're secretly afraid you'll never have any." I pump a fist. Nailed it.

"Right." Zoe nods. "But I do have a dog."

"A dog? Better make it a cat. I don't know anything about dogs."

"Okay. What kind of cat?"

I search my mind for cat breeds, but there's nothing there. "Okay, so not a cat either. Do you like fish?"

"What kind of fish?" Ugh. This is too much work.

"Can we come back to this?"

"It's your story," says Zoe.

We stop for a red light, jogging in place.

"I live in New Jersey," she volunteers.

"You do not. I haven't been to New Jersey since I was ten."

"You're going to need to do some research, then, because I definitely live in New Jersey."

"It's illegal to pump your own gas there, right?" This is

the only thing I know about her state.

"True," says Zoe.

I muse. "So maybe that's how you meet the guy."

As soon as I mention him, a man materializes on the other side of Zoe. His hair is solidly brown but the eyes flicker back and forth. Blue. Brown. Gray. Brown. I finally settle on brown. My husband has brown eyes.

The walk signal lights up, and the three of us jog over the crosswalk. "You must be… Malcolm? Or Charles?"

He shakes his head. "Owen."

"Zoe and Owen," I say aloud. A man walking his dog gives me a quizzical glance, but I'm lost in their names. "Too many long 'O' sounds," I tell the newcomer. "What else you got?"

"Damon. Waylon. Norman. Herman. Nolan."

"No."

"Joey!" says Zoe, and she and the guy exchange grins.

I give her a Look, then put my foot down. "Your name is Matt," I tell Matt.

"Not Matthias?" he says, wrinkling his nose.

"Just Matt. Matt West. Short and sweet. Easy to spell."

"I'm pretty sure Matt is short for Matthias," he says.

"Not in this story it isn't."

"Whatever. Do I work at a gas station in New Jersey?"

"I'm not staying in New Jersey," Zoe chimes in. "I'm driving through New York but I've never pumped gas."

"Have you never left the state?" I ask her incredulously. Is that believable?

"I'm young," Zoe says. "I'm going to college."

"Wait, what? I said preschool teacher."

But her face is already changing. The few laugh lines that have been there until now smooth out and her ponytail disappears, replaced by a short, flirty hairstyle.

"Well, now Matt is way too old for you," I grumble.

Zoe pouts. "Maybe he's my age but he didn't go to college because…"

Matt jumps in animatedly. "Because my mom—no wait, my aunt—got really sick, and there was no one to take care of her. So I have to pump gas to pay the bills." In an instant, his face loses a decade of wear as well as its light coating of facial hair.

"No one has a job pumping gas in New York," I remind him.

"Oh, for him, I'd stay in New Jersey," Zoe says.

There is a bench at the park just up ahead. "Hang on," I say, taking out my phone. "I need to write some of this stuff down."

I sit down in the middle of the bench, and Zoe and Matt plop down on either side of me. Opening my note-taking app, I thumb in their names, then begin to list the details we've established so far. As I hunch over my phone, the two of them talk across me.

"Maybe I don't work at the gas station," Matt says. "Maybe I work at the college, but you run into trouble pumping gas, and I happen to see you."

"And you jump into help because you're such a gentleman!"

"Yes, exactly! And you think you're never gonna see me again, but then…"

"You're serving quesadillas in the cafeteria!"

I type furiously, trying to get down every single idea as it comes. At this rate, I could have an outline by the end of the week, and then I could start the first draft.

I fight against autocorrect, which wants to change QUESADILLA to QUESTIONS, then sit back, waiting for more.

It only takes a second to realize I'm on the bench alone. In the distance, I see Zoe and Matt walking hand in hand.

"Wait!" I call out. They pause momentarily, and I wave, beckoning them back to me, but they don't even notice. Their lips meet in a kiss, and then they vanish altogether. I slump on the bench with a sigh as I realize I never even got a look at what they were wearing.

All the way home, I look for glimpses of my characters. Were Zoe's shoes blue or brown? What kind of pants did Matt have on? Or were they shorts?

A quarter mile from home, I give up, pop in my earbuds and turn up the music. Maybe they'll be back tomorrow.

Back at home, I grab some tea and toast for breakfast, then turn on the shower. If I don't wash my hair, I can be in and out in two minutes and get my work done with plenty of time to spare.

I've just stepped into the stream of water when there is a tug on the shower curtain and the sound of a man clearing his throat. I nearly slip, but catch myself before a fatal accident can occur.

"Who are you?" I ask.

"Seth," he says, and I rack my brain. Do I have a Seth? That doesn't sound like a name I'd use. But sometimes I pick something as a placeholder to be changed later.

"I can't place you." I wrap myself in the curtain liner and peer out at him. He blinks at me with long eyelashes and I gasp. "Your name's not Seth! You're Duncan." He's from the mystery novel I wrote last November. I haven't touched it since.

"Duncan is a name for a cat." He makes a face.

"Well… Seth rhymes with death," I shoot back. It's a weak argument, but the name-swapping is driving me up a wall.

"That's actually perfect," he says cheerily. "Because turns out—wait for it—I'm the murderer."

"For the love of—" I roll my eyes. I am not doing this. It took me forever to plot this book. No. I snap the shower curtain shut. I don't have time for this.

Silence falls, and I'm pretty sure he's gone when a paper clip appears at my feet, followed by a hair tie and a piece of string. I poke my head out to yell at Seth and see that his pants now have a million pockets, all of which are full of clues, all of which he seems determined to toss into my bathtub.

"I know you wanted it to be Taylor," he says, rummaging to the bottom of an especially deep pocket. "I get it. You like me, and you want me to be the good guy. But—" His hand emerges from his pocket holding a knife. He points it at me.

"Stop that," I scold. "This is starting to feel like a horror movie."

"But look," he says, holding the knife directly under my nose. I flinch, but my anxiety is quickly replaced by shock when I notice the dried drops of blood.

"Wait," I say. "Why does the knife have blood on it? The murder weapon was a shard of glass."

"Is that what you think? Man, I really am an evil genius."

I beam. I can't help it. He's charming. Is he seriously the murderer? He can't be the love interest and the murderer. Unless I switch genres? But I wasn't going to do anything with this book. I have other things to do. *Argh*.

I reach past Seth for my robe, then duck back into the shower to wrap myself in it. Once I'm decent, I step out onto the bathmat, carefully avoiding all the items now collecting beneath the faucet. As I step toward the sink, he drops the knife into the tub, too, and a brown swirl of blood washes down the drain.

"That's what I did," he says, pointing to the now-clean weapon. "I rinsed the knife so no one would suspect."

Is this a thing? I'll need to do some research. But not now. Now it's time for me to get serious about writing that column.

"Seth," I say. "I really don't have time for this now. Can't you come back later? I might have time on the weekend to dust off the manuscript and take a look."

"I may never come back," he says ominously. "This may be your only chance to finally finish the book with the perfect ending."

This is why, three hours later, despite having gotten up before dawn, I have accomplished nothing but a new outline of a mystery novel where every previous red herring is now a clue, Seth is probably the murderer, and there is no love interest. I remember now why I abandoned this genre. Thankfully, I am finally interrupted by a phone call, and Seth gathers up his crazy ideas and disappears.

Unfortunately, the phone call is from my boss, checking in on my progress. I quickly open a blank document on my laptop, then assure her that I am working on it right now.

It's not until the end of the work day, approaching the dinner hour, that I am interrupted again. I have a very rough draft assembled, so I take a break and start some soup. After adding the rice, I turn around and a chair that was empty a moment ago is now occupied by what appears to be a tiny pink piglet.

I groan. Is this a picture book idea? I don't want to write a picture book. Turning down the burner, I decide the best thing to do is to sit and ride out the brainstorm so that by the time my husband gets home, I'll be ready to revise my column. A grocery receipt and marker are handy, so I just snatch those up, ready to get this out of my system so I can get back to more important things.

The pig hops up on the chair beside me, opens its mouth, and says, "I'm Florunda."

Instantly I realize what this is. It's one of the three times a year I get the urge to write fantasy. If the talking pig hadn't tipped me off, the ridiculous name would have. I am notoriously terrible at fantasy names.

"Florunda from Flipovar?" I ask with a sigh.

"Flipovaria," she corrects me, and my shoulders slump. The extra syllables are not an improvement.

"Right, okay. And what kind of world is Flipovaria?"

Florunda changes color from typical barnyard pink to shimmering purple. Before I can blink, she sprouts wings. First they are tiny cherubic ones, but they quickly expand to a size worthy of a full-grown pegasus.

"Flipovaria is in the land of Forn," Florunda divulges

knowingly. "Where pigs fly."

I drop the marker. The cliches. Every time, the cliches. Why?

"Are you sure you don't do anything other than fly?"

"Well, we talk, but I thought that was obvious."

"No, but, like, do you dance?"

"In the clouds. All the time. We dance with our wings."

"That's still flying. Can you predict the future, maybe?"

"Why would a pig predict the future?"

"Why would a pig do anything?" I shoot back. "Why are you even a pig?"

Florunda's eyes go wide, and a second later so do mine, as her face contorts, first taking on the countenance of a goat, then a rhinoceros, a cow, a horse, a chicken, something that must be a dragon, and then a truly bizarre-looking creature with features from several of the previous iterations. I look down to see that in my shock I have drawn whatever it is, and it's actually kind of cute. Maybe Florunda's not a pig, but a… Fingungula. Yes, a Fingungula, which is an adorable purple little thing with wings that flies and dances in the clouds above the kingdom of Forn. Perfect.

Next to my drawing, I begin taking notes on the characteristics of Fingunguli until the receipt is entirely full of little chicken-scratch notes about legs and snouts and wings and color combinations. It's only when I run out of space that I realize there is no longer a pig or any other cute little purple animal sitting beside me. Florunda is gone and my husband has taken her place.

"What are you doodling?" he asks, sliding the receipt away from me before I can object. "Is this an owl?"

"What? No! It's a—" Shoot, I've already forgotten what I called it. Fungungler. Fandangley. Fruntuckle. I reach for my notes to remind myself of the spelling, but now I have no idea of the pronunciation. Is that G as in Gordon or as in George? What would a reader think? And is this a picture book? I really don't want to write a picture book.

"It's an owl," my husband says.

I drop my head to the table and tap my forehead against it twice. Who am I kidding? A bunch of F names and tiny purple flying creatures that resemble owls? This may be the shortest attack of fantasy writing in history, but I'm over it. I take the receipt paper with my scribble all over it and crumple it up.

"Where is Forn, anyway?" my husband asks, and I toss the rolled-up ball of paper at his head.

It's been a long day and I could not be happier for bedtime to finally arrive. I finished my column around seven, sent a few emails back and forth about some edits, and now there is nothing left to stand between me and my pillow.

I'm under the covers, the light is out, and my husband is already lightly snoring when a familiar voice sounds close to my ear.

"We are sooooo sorry," Zoe says. I pop one eye open. Oh, they're both here. Of course.

"We didn't mean to get so carried away," says Matthias. No, Matt. Matt. We're keeping this simple. "I'm just such a swoony male lead."

"You're no Seth," I mumble, but Matt and Zoe don't seem to hear.

"We're ready to talk now," Zoe says. "We've figured out how we meet, and why we can't be together. He's the teaching assistant for one of my classes."

"And she's failing." Matt laughs. "She's not dumb. She just doesn't get math."

I groan and begin groping blindly on the nightstand for a notebook. A book and a bracelet fall to the floor before I land on what I need.

In the meantime, Zoe prattles on with her entire life story. She's never been good at math because her fourth-grade teacher was mean to her about her multiplication tables, so then she had to be homeschooled, but some girl in her neighborhood bullied her so it was just as bad as going to school, and she has a phobia of tutors and—

You know what? No. I'm done for today. I wasted too much time on ideas I'm not going to use, and honestly, now that these two have come back once, I'm sure they'll come back again. This can wait until tomorrow morning when I'm ready to sit down and write.

Matt has just started detailing all of his aunt's medical treatments when I cut him off. "That's enough for now. Come back tomorrow."

"But he's just getting to the good part!" whines Zoe.

"Here." I grip the pen half-heartedly, and jot a couple of keywords on the notepaper. "See? Now I won't forget."

With twin shrugs, the lovebirds fade into a dark corner of the bedroom, and I drop my head back onto the pillow. Out of the brief silence comes a voice. "You mean like you forgot about me?"

I gasp, then grab the notebook, flipping back several pages. He was here a few nights ago. When I woke up the next day, I couldn't tell what I'd written. Pilot? Pilates? Now I know.

"Pirate!" I jab my finger at the page, and hold it up to show him.

"Ay. Mortimer Jones."

At the sound of his name, it all comes back to me, the sad tale of the lonely pirate on a quest to find his one true love. As I remember his trusty dolphin friend, I hear the slosh of water behind the closed bathroom door. Near the ceiling fan, there is a burst of rainbow colors, and I understand that it wasn't CARROT, but PARROT.

"Come on now," says Mortimer. "No time to waste. We'll be setting sail again in the morning."

I avoid looking at the glowing numbers of the bedside

clock, already ticking past ten, as I shove my feet into a pair of slippers and race down the stairs to find my laptop. It's going to be a long night.

Author Bios

In Story Order

Xanna Renae

Xanna Renae loves daydreaming about how to save her characters from the messes she puts them in. Currently she is giving life to the ideas inside her head from rural Missouri where she lives with her husband, Noah, and cat, Maestro. She has a bachelor of arts in Creative Writing from Southern New Hampshire University, where she graduated with honors.

When she isn't writing you can find her tucked away in her little bungalow reading, snuggling with her cat, or playing video games with her husband.

Her previous works include *Through the Violet Redwoods* and *The Willow Tree Swing.*

Find her online talking about writing, publishing, and life with chronic illnesses just about everywhere @XannasBooks or on her website XannaRenae.com

Willow Whitehead

Willow Whitehead has a love/hate relationship with writing, the words spill onto the page faster than she can type, or she'll stare at a blank document for hours. Though the words always come a bit easier in the middle of the night. Currently, she spends her days reading, drinking tea, and chasing her black cat, Z, through the woods.

You can follow her on Instagram as @WeepingWillowReviews and watch as she struggles to balance her time between work, rest, and her innumerable hobbies. Her previous publications include *The Willow Tree Swing* by Nightshade Publishing.

Abraham Vila

Abraham Vila is a 22-year-old Spanish author. He graduated in English Philology at the Complutense University of Madrid in 2023 and has always been passionate about reading and writing. One of his favourite books is Little Women and he loves quiet plans and travelling.

He can be found on Instagram as @_AbeVila

Kayla Whittle

Kayla Whittle works in acquisitions at a medical publisher. She has previously had short stories published in Luna Station Quarterly and The Colored Lens. She has stories in the anthologies Beyond the Veil (Ghost Orchid Press), Eros & Thanatos (Quill & Crow Publishing House), Of Fate & Fury (Silver Wheel Press), and Exquisite Poison (Phantom House Press), and has pieces included in Dangerous Waters: Deadly Women of the Sea and Daughter of Sarpedon: A Tempered Tales Collection, both out by Brigids Gate Press. Her work has also been featured on Flash Fiction Podcast. Much of her writing features queer representation, often including ace or sapphic characters. She can be found on Instagram as @CaughtBetweenThePages or on Twitter @kaylawhitwrites. When not writing, she's usually busy reading or planning her next Disney vacation. She currently lives in New Jersey.

Natasha Alva

Natasha Alva is currently a chemical engineering student who enjoys writing poems. Poetry became an unexpected hobby for her as she discovered it during the pandemic as a way to relieve stress from schoolwork and express bottled feelings. Through poetry, she gets to write stories and hopefully inspire people to appreciate literature in the form of writing. You can connect with Natasha on Instagram at @TheBuriedPages where she posts her poems. Some of her poems are currently featured in the Balm 2: Poetry for Beautifully Broken Souls and Magkasintahan 2.0 Volume VII.

Kristen Bazen

Kristen Bazen discovered the magic of the written word in elementary school. She completed her first novella in fifth grade and a novel in tenth grade (written while she was supposed to be studying or sleeping). Now, she mainly writes YA fantasy inspired by the Middle East and strong Christian themes. She also enjoys writing poetry to process difficult seasons and capture the wonder of life. Her poetry is featured in the anthologies The Heights We'll Fly To and Masquerade, and she has short stories published in The Willow Tree Swing and Wither and Bloom. When she's not working or writing, Kristen dabbles in languages, trains in martial arts, and raises awareness on how ordinary people can fight human trafficking. You can find her online at kristenbazen.com, or on Instagram as @Kristen_TheWriteEnding.

Hannah Carter

Hannah Carter is just a girl who loves to dream and write and still wakes up every day hoping to figure out she's secretly a mermaid. Her debut YA fantasy novel, Depths of Atlantis—filled with murder, magic, and, of course, mermaids—is out now through SnowRidge Press. Her short stories and award-winning flash fiction pieces have been published in over twenty anthologies. In 2022, her flash fiction piece, "A Home for Nova," won Havok's "Prismatic" anthology's Editors' Choice Award as well as a Realm Award. In addition to fiction, she also has had over a dozen devotionals published. In her spare time, she's probably either cuddling her cats, drinking tea, reading, or practicing for her imaginary Broadway debut. Connect with her on Instagram at @mermaidhannahwrites.

Miriam Stuart

Miriam is a new author in Cedar Springs, Michigan. She lives
with her husband Eli, and their two cats JarJar and Piglet.
In her spare time, Miriam enjoys working on her first novel,
thrifting, and creating delicious things in the kitchen. Miriam's
passions are deeply rooted in her Christian faith, relationships
with loved ones, and a desire to learn new things

Anne J. Hill

Anne J. Hill is an author who enjoys writing fantasy for all ages. Her love of words has led to her career as an editor and content writer. She runs Twenty Hills Publishing with the help of her circus performing best friend, Lara E. Madden. She spends her days dreaming up fantastical realms, researching ways to get away with murder…for writing, arguing over commas at the kitchen table, talking out loud to the characters in her head, promising her housemate that she isn't, in fact, crazy, and rearranging her personal library—affectionately dubbed the "Book Dungeon."

Katie Fitzgerald

Katie Fitzgerald is a trained children's librarian turned stay-at-home, homeschooling mom. Originally from the Hudson Valley in New York State, she now lives in Maryland with her librarian husband, four daughters, and one son. She has published two textbooks for librarians and is a monthly contributor to CatholicMom.com. Her flash fiction has appeared online at Spark Flash Fiction and Havok Publishing and in print in Wither and Bloom (Twenty Hills Publishing, 2023). When she's not writing humor or romance, she's usually listening to an audiobook at triple speed or buying used paperbacks to add to her to-be-read pile.

She can be found on Twitter as @MrsKatieFitz and on Instagram as @Read.At.Home.Mom

Acknowledgements

We would like to thank all of our authors for their wonderful submissions to this anthology. Without them, there would be no stories for us to share with you all.

We hope you've enjoyed this anthology, and that you look forward to future tales that Nightshade Publishing brings.

Thank You.